Anthony
and the Girls

Ole Könnecke

Anthony
and the Girls

Translated from the German by Nancy Seitz

Farrar, Straus and Giroux
New York

Here comes Anthony.

Anthony is cool.

Anthony has a bucket.

Anthony has a shovel.

Anthony has a
really big car.

But the girls don't look.

Anthony can jump high.

Anthony is strong.

Anthony can go
down the slide
headfirst,
on his stomach.

Eyes closed.

But the girls
still don't look.

Anthony is mad.

Anthony builds something.

Anthony builds a house.

Anthony builds the biggest
house in the world.

The house falls down.

Anthony cries.

Now the girls look.

Anthony gets a cookie.

Now Anthony can play
with the girls.

Anthony is happy.

Here comes Luke.

Copyright © by Carl Hanser Verlag München Wien 2004
Translation copyright © 2006 by Farrar, Straus and Giroux
All rights reserved
Originally published in Germany by Carl Hanser Verlag,
under the title *Anton und die Mädchen*
Distributed in Canada by Douglas & McIntyre Ltd.
Printed in the United States of America by Worzalla Publishing
First American edition, 2006
3   5   7   9   10   8   6   4   2

www.fsgkidsbooks.com

Library of Congress Control Number: 2005929250

ISBN-13: 978-0-374-30376-1
ISBN-10: 0-374-30376-2